7/10
1YF

12/12
14rt

D0105412

BOOK

Fiber

RICK BASS
Fiber

Illustrations by

Elizabeth Hughes Bass

The University of Georgia Press *Athens & London*

Published by the University of Georgia Press
Athens, Georgia 30602
© 1998 by Rick Bass
Illustrations © 1998 by Elizabeth Hughes Bass
All rights reserved
Set in Meridien
Printed and bound by RR Donnelley & Sons Company
The paper in this book meets the guidelines for
permanence and durability of the Committee on
Production Guidelines for Book Longevity of the
Council on Library Resources.

Printed in the United States of America
02 01 00 99 98 C 5 4 3 2 1

Library of Congress Cataloging in Publication Data

Bass, Rick, 1958–
Fiber / Rick Bass ; illustrations by Elizabeth Hughes Bass
p.   cm.
ISBN 0-8203-2063-3 (alk. paper)
ISBN 0-8203-2086-2 (sp. ed. : alk. paper)
I. Title.
PS3552.A8213F53   1998
813'.54—DC21   98-15556

British Library Cataloging in Publication Data available

For hope

I

When we came into this country, runaways, ren-
egades, we were like birds that had to sing. It was
only ten years ago but it feels like a hundred, or
maybe a thousand. No person can know what a
thousand years feels like, though in the first part
of my life, I was a geologist, and was comfortable
holding a foot-long core of earth and examining
such time—a thousand years per inch.

In the section of my life after that one, I was an
artist, a writer of brief stories, comfortable holding
a sheaf of ten or twelve pages in which a lifetime,
even several lifetimes, passed. A few thousand
people would read my slim books. They would
write letters to me then and talk about the charac-
ters in those stories as if they were real people,
which strangely saddened me.

Then came the third life. I became an activist. It

3

was as if some wall or dam burst within me, so that everything I wrote had to be asking for something—petition signatures, letters to Congress, etc.—instead of giving something.

But any landscape of significance, of power—whether dramatic or understated—will alter us, if we let it. And I am being bent yet again, though not without some fracturing; now I am into my fourth life, one that is built around things more immediate than the fairy-wing days of art. Even this narrative, this story, is fiction, but each story I tell feels like the last one I'll do—as if I've become like some insect or reptile trying to shed the husk of its old skin—and even now as I struggle toward the perceived freedom of the next phase of my life—the light ahead—neither you nor I can really be sure of how much of any story is fiction, or art, and how much of it is activism.

I am trying hard to move forward cleanly into the next territory. But still, things slip and fall back; the old, even when it is buried beneath the new, sometimes rises and surges, pierces through, and reappears.

4

Sometimes it feels as if I am running toward
the future, with a hunger for it, but other times, as
if I am simply fleeing the past, and those old skins.
It's so hard not to look back.

I cut sawlogs to sell to the mill. Prices are high on
the back end of an election year (low interest rates,
new housing starts), as the economies of man heat

to incandescence, fueled by China's child labor, Mexico's slave labor—fueled by the five-dollar-an-hour slave labor even in our own country—and in sawing those logs, the first thing I notice is whether the log I cut is an old tree or a young tree. I don't mean whether it's a big one or not; all the logs I cut are of roughly the same size—big enough so that I can almost get my arms around them. They are each a hundred inches long, a figure I can measure off in my sleep, or can pace blindfolded. I've cut so many hundred-inch logs that I tend to see the world now in hundred-inch increments. That's the size log the L-P mill over in Idaho needs for its laser mill, which makes short (eight-foot) two-by-fours. There's not a lot of waste. Those fucking lasers don't leave much kerf.

So the logs I cut are all about the same size, but each one is a different weight and density, based mostly on age, and based also on whether the tree got to be that big by growing quickly, or slowly.

The first cut you make into the log will show you this—will tell you just about all you'd ever want to know about that tree's history. I can handle larger individual logs, and sometimes I'll hump some big-ass honker, tight, green old-growth spruce or fir—four hundred fucking pounds packed into that hundred-inch length—but mostly I try to carry out only the medium-sized ones, which fill up the back of the truck quickly enough. Some of them will be eighty or ninety years old, if they grew slowly, in a shadowy light-starved place (the kind of woods where I best like to work in summer); and others, the same size, will be only twenty or thirty years old, with their growth rings spaced a quarter inch apart or wider—trees that are seemingly made up of liquid sunlight, trees like pipe straws sucking up water and sucking down sunlight, trees of no real integrity or use, weakened from having grown too fast, and without ever having been tested.

But I get paid for volume, not quality, and I load them into the truck too, a hundred inches at a time, though they feel light as balsa wood, after having just handled an eighty- or ninety-year-old log, and I feel guilty thinking of some carpenter

7

three thousand miles away—Florida, perhaps—
building some flimsy-shit house with those studs,
the wood splitting like parchment at the first tap of
a nail, and the carpenter cursing some unknowable
thing, groping with his curse to reach all the way
back to the point of origin, which is, what? The
mill? Me? The sunlight? The brutality of supply
and demand, and the omnipresent hypercapitalism
here at post-consumer century's end? Finish the
house, stucco over the mistakes, paint it bright red
and blue, sell the sonofabitch, and move on.
What're they going to do, dissect the house to
cross-examine each strut, each stud? Who knows
what's inside anything? More and more I'm trying
not to look back at who I was, or even who I am,
but at the land itself. I am trying to let the land tell
me who and what I am—trying to let it pace and
direct me, until it is as if I have become part of it.

This country—the Yaak Valley, way up in the
northwest tip of Montana—burns and rots, both.
The shape of the land beneath the forests is like the
sluggish waves in an ancient, nearly petrified

ocean—the waves of the northern Rockies sliding into the waves of the Pacific Northwest—so that it is like being lost, or like having found the rich dense place you were always looking for. You can walk around any given corner, and in less than a hundred paces go from fire-dependent ponderosa pine and grassland into the shadowy, dripping, mossy cedar-and-hemlock forests, rich with the almost sexual smell of rot. Tree frogs, electric-red salamanders, wood thrushes, ferns; climb a little farther, past the trickling waterfall, past the mossy-green skull of a woodland caribou, and you come to a small glacier, across which are sculpted the transient, sun-melting tracks where a wolverine passed by the day before. The tracks and scourings

of the glacier across the stone mountain, beneath all that ice, are only slightly less transient.

Down the sunny back side of the mountain, you can pass through one of the old 1910 burns, where there are still giant larch snags from that fire, each one a hollowed-out home to woodpeckers, martens, and bear cubs. This old burned-out forest still has its own peculiar vital force and energy and seems to almost *seethe*, drunk or intoxicated on the health of so much available sunlight, and drunk on the health of the rich fire-blackened soil—the nutritiousness of ashes.

Then, farther down the mountain, you'll be back into damp creek-side silent old growth: more moss, and that dark Northwest forest—spruce and fir.

Back home, in your cabin, your dreams swirl, as if you are still traveling, still walking, even in your sleep, across this blessed landscape, with all its incredible diversity, and the strength that brings.

In the first life, back in Louisiana, I took things. Just the oil, at first, from so deep beneath the ground, and from such a distant past that at the start it did not seem like a taking; but then, gradually and increasingly, from the surface.

I took boats, big boats, from their moorings at the marina at night: sailed them all night long—sometimes alone, other times with my wife, Hope. Before dawn we would sail back toward shore, then open the boat's drain plug to try to sink it, or sometimes would even torch the boat, and swim back in that last distance to shore, and then watch, for a while, in the darkness, the beautiful flaming spectacle of waste.

I would take everything, anything. The manhole covers to flood sewers in the street. License plates. Once, a sewing machine. From a backyard in suburban Lafayette, a picnic table. It was as if I was trying to eat the world, or that part of it. The newspapers began reporting the strange disappearances. They couldn't make rhyme or reason of it—there seemed no logic to it.

I went in through windows and from dresser tops took jewelry and other riches. I didn't ever sell anything: I just took it. It pleased me. I would

11

place the objects elsewhere. There are diamond necklaces hung in the boughs of cypress trees in Louisiana, pearl earrings in bird nests in the Atchafalaya.

I took cars: got in them and drove a short distance, then hid them, or sank them. It filled a need in me. I would look at my two hands and think, What are these made for, if not to take?

II

I believe in power. What I mean to say is I ascribe great value to it, and like to observe power in action. I like the way continents are always straining to break apart or ride up on and over one another, and I like the way the seedlings in the forest fight and scramble for light.

I like all that goes on in the hundred years of a tree's life, or the two hundred or five hundred years of its span—all the ice and snow, the windstorms, the fires that creep around the edges of some forests and sweep through and across others, starting the process all over, and leaving behind a holy kind of pause, a momentary break in power, before things begin to stretch and grow again, as vigorously as ever.

It feels good after sitting hunch-shouldered at a desk these last ten or twelve years to be hauling

real and physical things out of the woods: to get
the green sweet gummy sap of fir stuck to my
gloves and arms; to have the chunks of sawdust
tumble from the cuffs of my overalls; to have the
scent of the forest in my hair. The scent of leather
gloves. The weight of the logs as real as my brief
life, and the scent of blue saw smoke dense in my
leather boots. The sight of bright-cut, new yellow
pinewood—a color that soon fades as it oxidizes,

just as the skin of a gleaming fish fades quickly, immediately after it dies, or the hue of a river rock is lost forever after it is taken from the waters of its particular stream . . .

They can never find me. They have been up here looking for me—with warrants—and may come again, but I have only to slip into the woods and disappear for a while. And perhaps this is where the activism came from, after the storytelling—the desire to defend a land that defended me. The desire to give, for once, after a lifetime of taking. Perhaps one reason none of us knows what's inside the heart or core of anything is that it's always changing: that things are always moving in a wave, or along an arc, and that the presence of one thing or one way of being indicates only that soon another will be summoned to replace it, as the night carves out the next day.

I thought I was made all along for writing short stories, and maybe one day again I will be—as forests recycle through succession—but this landscape has carved and fit me—it is not I who have been doing the carving—and I can feel, am aware of, my change, so that now what I best fit doing is hauling logs, one at a time.

I'm short—a low center of gravity—with short legs, but long arms, and a heart and lungs that don't get tired easily. The red meat, the core of me, is stronger than ever. Certain accessories or trappings, such as ligaments, cartilage, disks, etc., are fraying and snapping—I get them mended, stitched back together, stapled and spliced or removed—but the rest of me is getting stronger, if slower, and I keep hauling the logs out one at a time, stepping gently over and around the fairy slippers and orchids, and choosing for my harvest only the wind-tossed or leaning trees, or the trees that are crowded too close together, or diseased. I try and select individual trees like notes of music. As one falls or is removed, others will rise, and with each cut I'm aware of this.

Art is selectivity—that which you choose to put in a story—and it's what you choose to leave out, too. This new life is still a kind of music, a kind of art, but it is so much more real and physical and immediate. It feels right to be doing this—hauling the logs out, carrying them over my shoulder one at a time like railroad ties, some as dense and old as if soaked with creosote, or green life: and the more I carry, the stronger and more compact I get—the better I fit this job. As I choose and select, I listen to that silent music all around me, faint but real, of what I am doing—not imagining, but *doing*.

Sometimes I work in the rotting areas, other times in the burns. I become smeared with charcoal, blackened myself as if altered, and that night heading home I will stop and bathe in a stream and become pale again under the fierce stars and will sometimes think about the days when I wrote stories, and then further back, about the days when I practiced geology, and then even further, to childhood and joy and wonder: but without question, these days I am a black beast moving slowly through magical woods, growing shorter each year under those logs, as each year a disk is removed— as if I am sinking deeper and deeper into the old rot of the forest, until soon I'll be waist-deep in the soil—and it is neither delicious nor frightening. It is only a fit.

A thing I do sometimes, when I have a log I'm really proud of, is to haul it out and carry it on my back and place it in the road next to some other logger's truck, or sometimes even in his truck, like a gift.

It is nothing more complex than trying to work myself out from under some imbalance of the past. It will take a long time.

People are curious about who's doing it—the log fairy, they call him—and here, too, I take precautions not to get caught. I haul the heaviest, densest logs I can handle.

I know I'll get back to hauling the balsa-wood logs from the fields of light. I know it's not going to make a difference, but I try to select only the densest, heaviest blown-down logs from the old forests of darkness, and I try to envision them, after their passage to Idaho, or Texas, or wherever they go, as standing staunch and strong within their individual houses' frameworks. I picture houses and homes getting stronger, one at a time—one board at a time—as they feed on my magical forest, and then I imagine those strong homes raising strong families, and that they will act like cells or cores scattered across the country—like little stars or satellites—that will help shore up the awful sagging national erosions here at century's end. It's a fantasy, to be sure, but you tell me which is more real: an idea, such as a stated passion or desire of one human's emotions—susceptible to the vagaries of the world, and fading through time—or a hundred-inch, 250-pound green juicy fir on one's mortal shoulder. You tell me which is fantasy and which is real.

I am so hungry for something real.

As I said, when we came up here to escape the law, we were artists: that second life. I breathed art—

inhaled it, as the timber companies are inhaling this forest's timber—and I exhaled it, too. It was easy to write stories, even poems. I don't know what I'm doing, telling this one—only for a moment, and one more time, it is as if I have stepped in a hole, or have put back on one of the old, dry coats shed from an earlier time.

It was like a pulse, back then. There was an electricity between me and the land, and there was one between Hope and the land, too, and one between Hope and myself.

I'd work in my notebooks, sitting out at the picnic table, the sunlight bright on that paper, my pen curlicuing words and shapes across that parchment like lichens spreading across the page in time-lapse warp speed—and Hope would paint landscapes with oils, as she had done down in the South.

Back then she had worked in greens and yellows and had always walked around with dried smears of it on her hands and face, so that she seemed of the land, and of the seasons, down there, as I tried to be—the incredibly fertile, almost eternal spring of greens and yellows, in the South—but then once we got up to this valley, the colors changed to blue fir, and blue rock, and to white glaciers, and white clouds; and those became the colors affixed to her body, the residue of her work. There are four distinct seasons up here, as if in some child's fairy-tale book, except that after the South's slow motion, the seasons in Yaak seem almost to gallop—the quick burning flash of dry brown heat, *August*, then an explosion of yellow and red, *October*, then more blue and white, blue and white, then winter's black-and-whiteness, seeming to last forever, but snatched away finally by the incandescence of true spring—and even now after a decade (the trees in the forest around us another inch larger in diameter, since that time), Hope is still searching to settle into the rhythms of this place— the fast rhythms on the surface, as well as the slower ones frozen in the rock below.

Between her chores of running the household and helping raise the children, I do not see much blue paint smeared on her, or any other color. And we just don't talk about art anymore. An overwhelming majority of the art we see discourages us, depresses us—no longer inspires us—and whether this is a failure within us, or within the artists of this age, we're not sure.

It seems like a hundred years, not ten, since we first came up here. Back then I would stumble through the forest, pretending to hunt—sometimes taking a deer or elk or grouse—but mostly just thinking about stories: about what had to be at stake, in any given story, and about the orthodox but time-tested critical progressions, or cyclings, of beginning, middle, and end, and about resolutions within a story, and epiphanies—all the old things. They were new to me then and seemed as fresh as if none of it had ever been done before.

I did not know the names of the things that I was walking past, or the cycles of the forests, or the comings and goings, lives and deaths, the migrations, of the animals. At night, hiking home after I'd traveled too far or been gone too long, I did not know the names of things by their scent alone, as I passed by them in the darkness.

Those kinds of things came to me, though, and are still coming, slowly, season after season, and year after year; and it is as if I'm sinking deeper into the earth, ankle-deep in mulch now. I keep trying to move laterally—am drawn laterally—but recently it has begun to feel as if perhaps the beginnings of some of my old desires are returning, my burrowing or diving tendencies: the pattern of my entering the ground vertically again, as I did when I was drilling for oil; desiring to dive again,

as if believing that for every emotion, every object, every landscape on the surface, there is a hidden or corresponding one at depth. We tend to think there are clean breaks between sections of anything, but it is so rarely that way, in either nature or our own lives: things are always tied together, as the future is linked, like an anchor, to the past.

Hope and I don't talk about art anymore. We talk about getting our firewood in for winter, or about

the deer we saw that day. We talk about the wild-
flowers, or the colors of leaves—that's the closest
we come to discussing the shadow or memory of
her work, and we do not come close to discussing
mine, either, or the memory or buried shadow of
it. We talk about *things,* instead, and hand things to

each other, for us to touch: a stone found on the
mountain that day, or an irregular piece of drift-
wood. A butterfly, wind-plastered and dried,
pinned to the grill of the truck, looking remarkably
like the silk scarves and blouses she would often
paint. We step carefully, desiring to travel further
into this fourth life: being pulled into it by un-
known or rather unseen rhythms. Walking quietly,
carefully, as if believing perhaps we can sneak

away from those old lives, and be completely free of them, and in pace—once more—with the land.

The logs that get you are almost always late in the day. You overextend, in your love, your passion for the work—the delicious physicality of it: the freedom of being able to work without acknowledging either a past or a future.

You spy a perfect fallen tree just a little bit out of your reach, and at the bottom of a steep slope. You have to cross a tangle of blowdown to get to it. It's a little larger than you should be carrying and a little too far from the truck—you've already hauled a day's worth—but all of these things conspire within you, as you stare at the log, to create a strange transformation or alteration: they reassemble into the reasons, the precise reasons, that you *should* go get that log.

And always, you do, so that you will not have to go to bed that night thinking about that log, and how you turned away from it.

III

There are seventy-six species of rare and endangered plants in this forest—Mingan Island moonwort, kidney-leaved violet, fringed onion, maidenhair spleenwort—and I know them all, each in both its flowering and dormant state. Most of them prefer the damp, dark depths of the last corners of old growth up here, though others prefer the ashes of a new fire, and appear only every two hundred years or so.

Still others seek the highest, windiest, most precarious existences possible, curled up in tiny clefts at the spartan tops of mountains, seeking brief moisture from the slow sun-glistening trickle of glaciers. I know all of them, and I watch carefully as I walk with the log across my back, across both shoulders like a yoke. Again it is like a slow and deliberate, plodding music—the music of

humans—choosing and selecting which step to place where, to avoid those seventy-six species, whenever I am fortunate enough to find any of them in the woods where I am working. They say the list is growing by a dozen or so each year. They say before it's all over, there won't be anything but fire ants and dandelions. They say . . .

That is my old life. This is my new one. My newest one. This one feels different—more permanent.

Still, the old one, or old ones, try to return. My right side's stronger than my left, so I use it more. By the end of the day it's more fatigued than the left, and it feels sometimes as if I'm being turned into a corkscrew; and because of this slight imbalance, accumulated and manifested over time, my steps take on a torque that threatens to screw me down deeper and deeper into the ground, like the diamond drill bits I'd fasten to the end of the pipe string when I worked in the oil fields. And late in the day I find myself once again daydreaming about those buried landscapes, and other hidden and invisible things.

A midnight run to town with four gleaming, sweet-smelling larch logs—hundred-inch lengths, of course, and each one weighing several hundred pounds. A cold night: occasional star showers, pulsings of northern lights, sky electricity. Coyote yappings, on the outskirts of town. A tarp thrown over the back of my truck, to hide the logs. One in one logger's truck, another in his neighbor's truck. So silent. They will think it is a strange dream when they look out in the morning and see the gift trees, the massive logs, but when they go out to touch them, they will be unable to deny the reality.

The third log into the back of yet another sleeping logger's truck, and the fourth one in the front yard of the mill itself, standing on end, as if it grew there overnight.

Home, then, to my wife and children and the pursuit of peace, and balance. In the winter, Hope and I sleep beneath the skins, the hides, of deer and elk from this valley.

There is an older lady in town who works on plow horses—gives them rubdowns, massages, hoists their hips and shoulders back into place when they pop out. She says they're easy to work with, that a horse won't tense up and resist you when you press or lean in against its muscles—and when my back gets way out of line, I go visit her, and she works on it. I lie there on her table by the woodstove while she grinds her elbow and knee into certain pressure points, and she pulls and twists, trying to smooth it all back into place, and she uses a machine she calls "Sparky," too, which I have never seen, because she uses it only on my back. It sends jolts of electricity deep into my muscles—which, she says, are but electrical fibers, like cables, conduits for electricity—and the sound that Sparky makes as she fires round after round of electricity into me (my legs and arms twitching like some laboratory frog's) is like that of a staple gun.

And sometimes I imagine that it is: that she is piecing me back together; that she is pausing, choosing and selecting which treatments to use on me that day, so that I can go back into the woods to choose and select which wood to take out and send to the faraway mills, who will then send the logs to . . .

We are all still connected, up here. Some of the connections are in threads and tatters, tenuous, but there is still a net of connectivity, through which magic passes.

Whenever a new car or truck enters the valley, I run and hide. I scramble to the top of a hill and watch through the trees as it passes. They can never get me. They would have to get the land itself.

The scent of sweat, of fern, of hot saw blade, boot leather, damp bark: I suck these things in like some starving creature. All the books in my house now sit motionless and unexamined on their shelves, like the photos of dead relatives, dearly loved and deeply missed. Sometimes I pull them down, touch the spines, even say their names aloud, as one would the name of one's mother, "Mom," or one's grandmother, "Grandma."

But then I go back out into the woods.

Once, carrying a log across a frozen pond, I punched through the ice and fell in up to my chest—the cold water such a shock to my lungs that I could barely breathe—and I had to drop the log and skitter out, then build a quick fire to warm up. (The heater in my old truck doesn't work.) Some days, many days, it feels like two steps forward, two steps back, as the land continues to carve and scribe us at its own pace.

And now when I take my pickup truck to the mill, and off-load my logs next to the millions of board feet that are streaming through it like diarrhea through a bloated pig's butt in the feedlot—what difference do I think it will make? How does my fantasy stand up then, under the broad examination of reality?

In protest, I haul the logs more slowly than ever.

In protest, I take more time with them. I touch them, smell them. I tithe the best ones to strangers. Sometimes I sit down and read the cross section of each log, counting the growth rings. Here is where one seedling grew fast, seeking light, struggling for co-dominance. Here is where it reached the canopy and was then able to put more of its energy into girth and width rather than height—stability. Here—this growth ring—is the drought year; then the succession of warm, wet growing years. Here— the next band of rings—is where the low-intensity fire crept through around the forest, scorching the edges of but not consuming the tree.

I read each of the logs in this manner, as if reading the pages of some book. Maybe someday I will go back to books. Maybe someday I will submerge back into the vanished or invisible world, and will live and breathe theory, and maybe Hope will start painting again.

But right now I am hauling logs, and she is gardening, raking the loose earth with tools, though other times with her bare hands, and it feels like we are falling, and as if we are starving, and as if I must keep protesting, must keep hauling logs.

We try not to buy *anything* anymore—especially anything made of wood. It's all such utter, flimsy shit. One touch, one stress on it, and it all splinters to hell—a hammer or ax handle, a stepladder, a chest of drawers . . . It is all such hollow shit, and we are starving.

Before I burned out in that third life, I was asizzle. I remember awakening each morning to some burning smell within me—scorched metal against metal. Manatees, ivory-billed woodpeckers, whales, wolves, bears, bison—I burned for it all, and did so gladly. The forest loves its fires.

The reason I think I left the second life—left art, left storytelling—was because it had become so safe, so submerged. It wasn't radical enough. They say most people start out being radical and then gravitate toward moderation, and then beyond moderation to the excesses of the right, but for me it has been the opposite—as if the land itself up here is inverted, mysterious, even magical, turning humans, and all else, inside out, in constant turmoil, constant revolution.

We—all painters and writers—don't want to be political. We want to be pure, and *artistic.* But we all know, too, I think, that we're not up to the task. What story, what painting, does one offer up to refute Bosnia, Somalia, the Holocaust, Chechnya, China, Afghanistan, or Washington, D.C.? What story or painting does one offer up or create to counterbalance the ever-increasing sum of our destructions? How does one keep up with the pace? Not even the best among us are up to this task, though each tries; like weak and mortal wood under stress, we splinter, and try to act, create, heal. Some of us fall out and write letters to Con-

gress, not novels; others write songs, but they are
frayed by stress and the imbalance of the fight.
Some of us raise children, others raise gardens.
Some of us hide deep in the woods and learn the
names of the vanishing things, in silent, stubborn
protest.

I want to shock and offend. Hauling *logs?* My
moderation seems obscene in the face of what is
going on on this landscape, and in this country—
the things, the misery, for which this country is so
much the source, rather than a source of healing
or compassion.

Paint me a picture or tell me a story as beautiful
as other things in the world today are terrible. If
such stories and paintings are out there, I'm not
seeing them.

I do not fault our artists for failing to keep up with, or hold in check, the world's terrors. These terrors are only a phase, like a fire sweeping across the land. Rampant beauty will return.

In the meantime, activists blink on and off like fireflies made drowsy over pesticide meadows. Activism is becoming the shell, the husk, where art once was. You may see one of them chained to a gate, protesting yet another Senate-spawned clearcut, and think the activist is against something, but the activist is for something, as artists used to be. The activist is for a real and physical thing, as the artist was once for the metaphorical; the activist, or brittle husk-of-artist, is for life, for sensations, for senses deeply touched: not in the imagination, but in reality.

The activist is the emergency-room doctor trying to perform critical surgery on the artist. The activist is the artist's ashes.

And what awaits the activist's ashes: peace?

IV

There is, of course, no story: no broken law back in Louisiana, no warrant, no fairy logs. I am no fugitive, other than from myself. Here, the story falls away.

It—storytelling—has gotten so damn weak and safe. I say this not to attack from within, only to call a spade a spade: a leftover lesson from art. I read such shit, and see such shit paintings, that I want to gag; one could spray one's vomit across the canvas and more deeply affect or touch the senses—what remains of them—than the things that are spewing out into the culture now.

The left has vanished, has been consumed by the right. On one day, the Sierra Club announces it is against all logging on national forests—"zero cut"—and the next day it turns around and endorses the re-election of President Clinton, who has just endorsed the industrial liquidation of five billion board feet of timber in one year alone. Hell, yes, employment is up, this year; what about after the election, when the five billion drops back to zero because it's all been cut or washed away by erosion? Clinton tosses in the Tongass National Forest in Alaska—old-growth coastal rain forest—gives the timber company a hundred-year lease on it. And the Sierra Club, bastion of radicalism, endorses him.

Trying to shore up his base among the environmentalists—a long, nasty word for which we should start substituting "human fucking beings"—Clinton designates a couple million acres of Utah desert as a national monument; the year before, he signed a Senate bill protecting California desert. He's made moves in the direction of protecting some Pacific Northwest old growth, too, but nothing for the Yaak; whether planned or not, he is making a political trade of rock for timber—trading the currency of the Yaak's wildness for votes and red rock—and this is an alteration, a transformation, that will not bear scrutiny; it is not grounded in reality, it cannot be done, it is superficial, flimsy, it is theft. He is not the environmental President. He is trading rock for timber. Each has its inherent values, but each is different.

The Yaak, perched up on the Canadian line like some hunch-shouldered griffin high in a snag looking down on the rest of the American West, can act as a genetic pipeline to funnel its wild creatures and their strange, magical blood down into Yellowstone and the Bitterroot country, and back out toward the prairies, too. It can still resurrect wildness. There is still a different thrumming in the blood of the Yaak's inhabitants.

The Nature Conservancy won't even get involved up here. The timber companies own the land along the river bottoms in the Yaak, and they clear-cut those lands and left town rather than wait for the trees to grow back as they're always bragging they'll do: but before leaving town (shutting down the mill behind them, so that now we have to export our wood, and jobs, to Idaho), the timber companies subdivided the hell out of those clear-cut lands, turned them into ranchettes, like cow turds all up and down the river, and still I couldn't get the Conservancy to become active up here.

When I wrote to them, they wrote back and told me the valley wasn't important enough. They hadn't ever even seen the damn place. Now the vice president of the timber company—Plum Creek—that's selling off these lands in such tiny fragments sits on the board of directors of the Nature Conservancy's Montana Chapter.

I don't mean to speak ill of anyone, and certainly not of a man I've never met, but Plum Creek's got tens of thousands of acres in the south end of the Yaak, in the Fisher River country, which is the only route by which a wandering grizzly can pass down out of the Yaak and into the rest of the West.

Plum Creek owns the plug, the cork, to the bottleneck—these lands were given away by Congress more than a hundred years ago—and so now the situation is that one man—one human, more heroic than any artist or group of artists ever dreamed of being—will do either the right thing, and protect that land, or the wrong thing, and strangle the last wildness.

If you think I'm going to say *please* after what they've already done to this landscape, you can think again. It is not about being nice or courteous. It is not even about being radical. It is simply about right versus wrong, and about history: that which has already passed, and that which is now being written and recorded.

I can hear my echo. I recognize the tinny sound of my voice. I know when an edge is crossed, in art: when a story floats or drifts backward or forward, beyond its natural confines. And I understand I am a snarling wolverine, snapping illogically at everything in my pain, snapping at everyone—at fellow artists, and at fellow environmentalists.

I am going to ask for help, after all. I have to ask for help. This valley gives and gives and gives. It has been giving more timber to the country, for the last fifty years, than any other valley in the Lower 48, and still not one acre of it is protected as wilderness.

I load the logs slowly into the back of my ragged truck and drive them slowly to the mill in protest. The valley cannot ask for anything—can only give—and so like a shell or husk of the valley I am doing the asking, and I am saying please, at the same time that I am saying, in my human way, fuck you.

Somebody help. Please help the Yaak. Put this story in the President's, or Vice President's, hands. Or read it aloud to one of them by firelight on a snowy evening with a cup of cider within reach, resting on an old wooden table.

The firelight on the spines of books on the shelf

flickering as if across the bones or skeletons of things; and outside, on that snowy night, the valley holding tight to the eloquence of a silence I can no longer hear over the roar of my own saw.

Somebody please do this. Somebody please help.

Acknowledgments

Montana is a vast state and relatively unpeopled. There are dozens of community-based conservation organizations spread thin across an at-times troubled land. Nearly every watershed, every valley, every forest or grove has a handful of activists working on its behalf. The last thing anyone has, in this day and age of increased pace, is spare time, and then beyond that, spare time to give to a place-beyond-one's-own. Nonetheless, that's what I'm asking for. And it's gratifying to see a slowly growing number of groups and individuals paying more attention to the Yaak Valley—to this unique biological treasure. I'm grateful to all of them for work done on the valley's behalf and for work to be done in the future. Every letter written, every tedious meeting attended—these seemingly useless efforts will have a cumulative effect that will yet be successful.

I'm grateful to the *Mississippi Review,* which first published "Fiber"; to Joe Barbato and Lisa Horak of the Nature Conservancy; and to Ethan Nosowsky at Farrar, Straus & Giroux, who published the story in a collection entitled *Off the Beaten Path: Stories of Place*—an anthology of fiction on behalf of America's remaining wild ecosystems.

I am grateful to Mike Branch, Scott Slovic, and the Association for the Study of Literature and Environment (ASLE) for their support of this story (and the Yaak) and to Barbara Ras and the University of Georgia Press for the same. I am grateful to my wife, Elizabeth, for the drawing and placement of the illustrations, and to Russell Chatham for the painting on the cover.

I'm grateful to my family, friends, and neighbors. I'm grateful to the wild Yaak itself. We all love it as it was and as it now is, and we all want it to stay as much the same as it is; among us there are variations only in our visions of how to best achieve that goal, that protection against the future's hunger. I complain often that activism distracts from fiction writing, but I will always be grateful for the valley and its wild inhabitants, for its four seasons, and for hope. Whenever I lose it, I have only to step into the deep woods, or climb to a mountaintop and feel the different winds, or lie down beneath a cool bower and press myself against the orange mulch of rot, to know hope again.

What You Can Do

There are two types of landowners in the Yaak: public and private. Protection of the available private Plum Creek lands is a complex and as-yet-unsolved dream, though protection of the last roadless cores of the public lands can be done for free. You can write to the White House, to Congress, and to Forest Service personnel, asking that they protect the last roadless cores of the Yaak Valley as wilderness.

The Yaak Valley Forest Council (918 Mineral Ave. #220, Libby, Montana 59923) advocates keeping the last roadless areas as they are—roadless—and also advocates local, sustainable logging, using only areas where roads already exist. The group would benefit greatly from donations, as would the nonprofit, tax-exempt Round River Conservation Studies (430l Emigration Canyon, Salt Lake City, Utah 84108), which has been working on conservation issues in the Yaak for several summers.

Dollars are useful, but letters to Congress—pleas, entreaties, demands—are what's needed most. I believe letters are more powerful than money: maybe just barely, but they are, if in sufficient and sustained quantity. Please write a letter testifying to your desire that the last roadless cores of the Yaak, and places like it, remain wild for all time, and send a copy of your letter to the following addresses:

President Bill Clinton
The White House
1600 Pennsylvania Ave.
Washington DC 20500

Vice President Al Gore
Old Executive Office Bldg.
Washington DC 20500

Senator Max Baucus
U.S. Senate
Washington DC 20510

Senator Conrad Burns
U.S. Senate
Washington DC 20510

Representative Sherwood
    Boehlert
U.S. House
Washington DC 20515

Representative Rick Hill
U.S. House
Washington DC 20515

Dan Glickman
Secretary of Agriculture
14th St. & Independence
Washington DC 20250

Jim Lyons
Department of Agriculture
14th St. & Independence
Washington DC 20250

Mike Dombeck
Chief, U.S. Forest Service
Box 96090
Washington DC 20090

Katie McGinty
Council on Environmental
    Quality
Old Executive Office Bldg.,
    Rm. 360
Washington DC 20501

Governor Marc Racicot
State Capitol
Helena MT 59620

Dale Bosworth
Regional Forester
Box 7669
Missoula MT 59807

Other organizations that have been active for many years on behalf of the vanishing public wildlands in Montana are the Montana Wilderness Association (P.O. Box 635, Helena, Montana 59624) and the Cabinet Resources Group (P.O. Box 238, Heron, Montana 59844). Their spirited support of this cherished homeplace has been greatly appreciated and is a service provided not just for local residents but on behalf of all citizens; we all possess a "stake" in these public wildlands. Groups such as these have been fighting a losing battle for many, many years, often in most inhospitable political environments, and I applaud their courage and perseverence.

Regular updates on national forestry issues concerning the Yaak can be found on the Internet at http://www.geocities.com/RainForest/Vines/5054.

A portion of the royalties from the regular edition of this book and all of the author's proceeds from the sales of the limited edition will go to Round River Conservation Studies to support their work in the Yaak.

About the Author and the Artist

RICK BASS is the author of numerous books of fiction and nonfiction, including *The Book of Yaak* (essays) and, most recently, the novel *Where the Sea Used to Be.* He is a board member of Round River Conservation Studies and of the Cabinet Resources Group, a council member of the Montana Wilderness Association, a member of the advisory board of the Association for the Study of Literature and Environment, and a member of the Yaak Valley Forest Council and of the Kootenai Forestry Congress. He lives in northwest Montana with his wife, the artist Elizabeth Hughes Bass, and their daughters.

While raising two children, ELIZABETH HUGHES BASS paints silk scarves and clothing and does watercolors and ink drawings.